This book is a love letter to all the wonderful kids out there. Wishing your heart bursts with happiness!

If you had a blast with our coloring book, leave us an Amazon review!

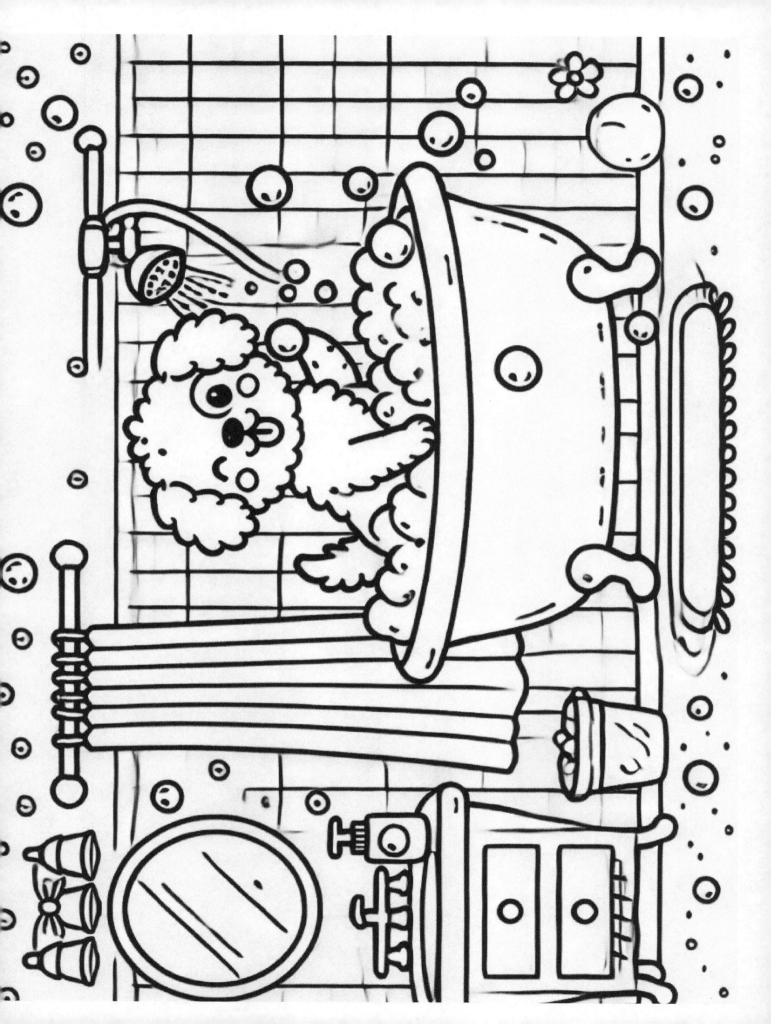

A Note From the Publisher

As a child, I absolutely loved coloring and found it incredibly creative. As an adult who frequently traveled for work, coloring became a fantastic way for me to de-stress in the evenings. I hope you'll enjoy this coloring book and find it as relaxing and inspiring as I have. If you have any suggested themes or feedback, please email me at tamera@boundlesscreations.org. Happy coloring!

Warm regards,

Tamera
Boundless Creations LLC

Made in the USA
Las Vegas, NV
20 December 2024

14937513R00059